CW00419879

To Be Read By Candlelight

To Be Read By Candlelight

TWO TALES OF SUSPENSE

BY

Edith Wharton

Þ

PARSIMONY PRESS
2000

This edition first published in the UK in 2000
Second impression 2000
Parsimony Press Ltd
West Huntspill, Somerset

Introduction and selection copyright
© Parsimony Press Ltd, 2000

ISBN 1 902979 09 5

Typesetting by Russell Enterprises
Printed and bound by Poligrafico Dehoniano, Italy

Many of the novelists we revere today cut their teeth on the short story. They were published by magazines and periodicals, eagerly awaited and devoured by a reading public living without the distraction of televisions, radios or playstations.

Edith Wharton was no exception. Although she is best known today for her novels and novellas, The Age of Innocence, The Custom of the Country and Ethan Frome to name but a few, she had been writing short stories for a decade before her first novel, the 30,000 copy bestseller The House of Mirth was published in 1905.

Of the eighty-odd short stories she produced over her lifetime, a substantial proportion were ghost stories, or had a creepy 'shivers down the spine' element to them. Strangely, she admitted to being terrified by the genre, and had burned a collection of ghost stories because she was too terrified to sleep knowing the book was in the house. (Stephen King has, apparently, made a similar confession about sometimes having to sleep with the light on).

When these stories were first published, the settings and characters were much more familiar to their readers than they are to us around a century later. Losing this immediacy may take the edge off our fear, but they are still page-turners. Edith Wharton remains today, as she was then, a great story-teller.

She was born Edith Newbold Jones in 1862. Her parents, George and Lucretia Jones, were rich and part of the New York elite. Her position was enviable. By the time she was 19 she was a well-educated, well-travelled and wealthy woman in her own right.

Her education was not wasted. She was bright and a voracious reader from an early age. It is ironic that although her parents were partly responsible for this by educating her so well, they were disturbed by it. The ambitions and expectations they harboured on her behalf were more concerned with her social position— a career as a writer would have been 'menial'.

She buckled down. In 1885 she married Teddy Wharton, a Boston socialite some years older than she was. It was not a success. With little in common and no 'grand passion' to bind them, she turned to writing. Slow at first, it was interrupted by a breakdown in her late thirties. After her recovery, stories and novels followed thick and fast (and to international acclaim).

She became a protegée and friend to Henry James, whom she greatly admired, but her closest friend was Walter Berry. He had been an early admirer, but had never proposed (forever remaining a bachelor). His involvement in her writing and companionship throughout her life must have made some amends for her marriage.

Her love life was pretty much barren, apart from a passionate, but brief, affair she had in her forties with an American journalist, William Morton Fullerton, who James had introduced her to in Paris.

1910 saw her move permanently to France with Teddy, from whom she finally divorced three years later. She was almost immediately thrown into the war. She was honoured by her adoptive country for her pragmatic efforts at relieving some of the suffering it brought.

She wrote until her death in 1937 and is buried in a cemetery in Versailles, close to her friend Walter Berry.

The Triumph of Night

I

I**T WAS CLEAR THAT THE SLEIGH FROM WEYMORE**
had not come; and the shivering young traveller
from Boston, who had counted on jumping into it
when he left the train at Northridge Junction, found
himself standing alone on the open platform, exposed
to the full assault of night-fall and winter.

The blast that swept him came off New Hampshire
snowfields and ice-hung forests. It seemed to have
traversed interminable leagues of frozen silence, filling
them with the same cold roar and sharpening its edge
against the same bitter black-and-white landscape.
Dark, searching and sword-like, it alternately muffled
and harried its victim, like a bull-fighter now whirling
his cloak and now planting his darts. This analogy
brought home to the young man the fact that he himself had no cloak, and that the overcoat in which he
had faced the relatively temperate air of Boston
seemed no thicker than a sheet of paper on the bleak
heights of Northridge.

George Faxon said to himself that the place was
uncommonly well-named. It clung to an exposed ledge
over the valley from which the train had lifted him,
and the wind combed it with teeth of steel that he
seemed actually to hear scraping against the wooden
sides of the station. Other building there was none:
the village lay far down the road, and thither—since
the Weymore sleigh had not come—Faxon saw himself under the necessity of plodding through several
feet of snow.

He understood well enough what had happened: his hostess had forgotten that he was coming. Young as Faxon was, this sad lucidity of soul had been acquired as the result of long experience, and he knew that the visitors who can least afford to hire a carriage are almost always those whom their hosts forget to send for. Yet to say that Mrs Culme had forgotten him was too crude a way of putting it. Similar incidents had led him to think that she had probably told her maid to tell the butler to telephone the coachman to tell one of the grooms (if no one else needed him) to drive over to Northridge to fetch the new secretary; but on a night like this, what groom who respected his rights would fail to forget the order?

Faxon's obvious course was to struggle through the drifts to the village, and there rout out a sleigh to convey him to Weymore; but what if, on his arrival at Mrs Culme's, no one remembered to ask him what this devotion to duty had cost? That, again, was one of the contingencies he had expensively learned to look out for, and the perspicacity so acquired told him it would be cheaper to spend the night at the Northridge inn, and advise Mrs Culme of his presence there by telephone. He had reached this decision, and was about to entrust his luggage to a vague man with a lantern, when his hopes were raised by the sound of bells.

Two sleighs were just dashing up to the station, and from the foremost there sprang a young man muffled in furs.

'Weymore?—No, these are not the Weymore sleighs.'

The voice was that of the youth who had jumped to the platform—a voice so agreeable that, in spite of the words, it fell consolingly on Faxon's ears. At the same moment the wandering station-lantern, casting a transient light on the speaker, showed his features to

be in the pleasantest harmony with his voice. He was
very fair and very young—hardly in the twenties,
Faxon thought—but his face, though full of a morning
freshness, was a trifle too thin and fine-drawn, as
though a vivid spirit contended in him with a strain of
physical weakness. Faxon was perhaps the quicker to
notice such delicacies of balance because his own tem-
perament hung on lightly quivering nerves, which yet,
as he believed, would never quite swing him beyond a
normal sensibility.

'You expected a sleigh from Weymore?' the new-
comer continued, standing beside Faxon like a
slender column of fur.

Mrs Culme's secretary explained his difficulty,
and the other brushed it aside with a contemptuous
'Oh, *Mrs Culme*!' that carried both speakers a long
way toward reciprocal understanding.

'But then you must be—' the youth broke off with a
smile of interrogation.

'The new secretary? Yes. But apparently there are
no notes to be answered this evening.' Faxon's laugh
deepened the sense of solidarity which had so
promptly established itself between the two.

His friend laughed also. 'Mrs Culme,' he explained,
'was lunching at my uncle's to-day, and she said you
were due this evening. But seven hours is a long time
for Mrs Culme to remember anything.'

'Well,' said Faxon philosophically, 'I suppose that's
one of the reasons why she needs a secretary. And I've
always the inn at Northridge,' he concluded.

'Oh, but you haven't, though! It burned down
last week.'

'The deuce it did!' said Faxon; but the humour of
the situation struck him before its inconvenience. His
life, for years past, had been mainly a succession of
resigned adaptations, and he had learned, before

dealing practically with his embarrassments, to extract from most of them a small tribute of amusement.

'Oh well, there's sure to be somebody in the place who can put me up.'

'No one *you* could put up with. Besides, Northridge is three miles off, and our place—in the opposite direction—is a little nearer.' Through the darkness, Faxon saw his friend sketch a gesture of self-introduction. 'My name's Frank Rainer, and I'm staying with my uncle at Overdale. I've driven over to meet two friends of his, who are due in a few minutes from New York. If you don't mind waiting till they arrive, I'm sure Overdale can do you better than Northridge. We're only down from town for a few days, but the house is always ready for a lot of people.'

'But your uncle—?' Faxon could only object, with the odd sense, through his embarrassment, that it would be magically dispelled by his invisible friend's next words.

'Oh, my uncle—you'll see! I answer for *him*! I daresay you've heard of him—John Lavington?'

John Lavington! There was a certain irony in asking if one had heard of John Lavington! Even from a post of observation as obscure as that of Mrs Culme's secretary the rumour of John Lavington's money, of his pictures, his politics, his charities and his hospitality, was as difficult to escape as the roar of a cataract in a mountain solitude. It might almost have been said that the one place in which one would not have expected to come upon him was in just such a solitude as now surrounded the speakers—at least in this deepest hour of its desertedness. But it was just like Lavington's brilliant ubiquity to put one in the wrong even there.

'Oh, yes, I've heard of your uncle.'

'Then you *will* come, won't you? We've only five

minutes to wait,' young Rainer urged, in the tone
that dispels scruples by ignoring them; and Faxon
found himself accepting the invitation as simply as it
was offered.

A delay in the arrival of the New York train length-
ened their five minutes to fifteen; and as they paced
the icy platform Faxon began to see why it had seemed
the most natural thing in the world to accede to his
new acquaintance's suggestion. It was because Frank
Rainer was one of the privileged beings who simplify
human intercourse by the atmosphere of confidence
and good humour they diffuse. He produced this
effect, Faxon noted, by the exercise of no gift but his
youth, and no art but his sincerity; and these qualities
were revealed in a smile of such sweetness that Faxon
felt, as never before, what Nature can achieve when she
deigns to match the face with the mind.

He learned that the young man was the ward, and
the only nephew of John Lavington, with whom he
had made his home since the death of his mother, the
great man's sister. Mr Lavington, Rainer said, had
been 'a regular brick' to him—'But then he is to every-
one, you know'—and the young fellow's situation
seemed in fact to be perfectly in keeping with his
person. Apparently the only shade that had ever rested
on him was cast by the physical weakness which Faxon
had already detected. Young Rainer had been threat-
ened with tuberculosis, and the disease was so far
advanced that, according to the highest authorities,
banishment to Arizona or New Mexico was inevitable.
'But luckily my uncle didn't pack me off, as most
people would have done, without getting another
opinion. Whose? Oh, an awfully clever chap, a young
doctor with a lot of new ideas who simply laughed at
my being sent away, and said I'd do perfectly well in
New York if I didn't dine out too much, and if I

dashed off occasionally to Northridge for a little fresh
air. So it's really my uncle's doing that I'm not in
exile—and I feel no end better since the new chap told
me I needn't bother.' Young Rainer went on to confess
that he was extremely fond of dining out, dancing and
similar distractions; and Faxon, listening to him, was
inclined to think that the physician who had refused
to cut him off altogether from these pleasures was
probably a better psychologist than his seniors.

'All the same you ought to be careful, you know.'
The sense of elder-brotherly concern that forced the
words from Faxon made him, as he spoke, slip his
arm through Frank Rainer's.

The latter met the movement with a responsive
pressure. 'Oh, I *am:* awfully, awfully. And then my
uncle has such an eye on me!'

'But if your uncle has such an eye on you, what
does he say to your swallowing knives out here in this
Siberian wild?'

Rainer raised his fur collar with a careless gesture.

'It's not that that does it—the cold's good for me.'

'And it's not the dinners and dances? What is it
then?' Faxon good-humouredly insisted; to which his
companion answered with a laugh: 'Well my uncle
says it's being bored; and I rather think he's right!'

His laugh ended in a spasm of coughing and a
struggle for breath that made Faxon, still holding his
arm, guide him hastily into the shelter of the fireless
waiting room.

Young Rainer had dropped down on the bench
against the wall and pulled off one of his fur gloves to
grope for a handkerchief. He tossed aside his cap and
drew the handkerchief across his forehead, which was
intensely white, and beaded with moisture, though his
face retained a healthy glow. But Faxon's gaze
remained fastened to the hand he had uncovered: it

was so long, so colourless, so wasted, so much older than the brow he passed it over.

'It's queer—a healthy face but dying hands,' the secretary mused: he somehow wished young Rainer had kept on his glove.

The whistle of the express drew the young men to their feet, and the next moment two heavily-furred gentlemen had descended to the platform and were breasting the rigour of the night. Frank Rainer introduced them as Mr Grisben and Mr Balch, and Faxon, while their luggage was being lifted into the second sleigh, discerned them, by the roving lantern-gleam, to be an elderly grey-headed pair, of the average prosperous business cut.

They saluted their host's nephew with friendly familiarity, and Mr Grisben, who seemed the spokesman of the two, ended his greeting with a genial—'and many more of them, dear boy!' which suggested to Faxon that their arrival coincided with an anniversary. But he could not press the enquiry, for the seat allotted him was at the coachman's side, while Frank Rainer joined his uncle's guests inside the sleigh.

A swift flight (behind such horses as one could be sure of John Lavington having) brought them to tall gateposts, an illuminated lodge, and an avenue on which the snow had been levelled to the smoothness of marble. At the end of the avenue the long house loomed up, its principal bulk dark, but one wing sending out a ray of welcome; and the next moment Faxon was receiving a violent impression of warmth and light, of hot-house plants, hurrying servants, a vast spectacular oak hall like a stage-setting, and, in its unreal middle distance, a small figure, correctly dressed, conventionally featured, and utterly unlike his rather florid conception of the great John Lavington.

The surprise of the contrast remained with him

through his hurried dressing in the large luxurious
bedroom to which he had been shown. 'I don't see
where he comes in,' was the only way he could put it,
so difficult was it to fit the exuberance of Lavington's
public personality into his host's contracted frame
and manner. Mr Lavington, to whom Faxon's case
had been rapidly explained by young Rainer, had
welcomed him with a sort of dry cordiality that exactly
matched his narrow face, his stiff hand, and the whiff
of scent on his evening handkerchief. 'Make yourself at
home—at home!' he had repeated, in a tone that suggested on his own part, a complete inability to perform
the feat he urged on his visitor. 'Any friend of Frank's
… delighted … make yourself thoroughly at home!'

II

In spite of the balmy temperature and complicated
conveniences of Faxon's bedroom, the injunction was
not easy to obey. It was wonderful luck to have found
a night's shelter under the opulent roof of Overdale,
and he tasted the physical satisfaction to the full. But
the place, for all its ingenuities of comfort, was oddly
cold and unwelcoming. He couldn't have said why,
and could only suppose that Mr Lavington's intense
personality—intensely negative, but intense all the
same—must in some occult way, have penetrated
every corner of his dwelling. Perhaps, though, it was
merely that Faxon himself was tired and hungry, more
deeply chilled than he had known till he came in from
the cold, and unutterably sick of all strange houses,
and of the prospect of perpetually treading other
people's stairs.

'I hope you're not famished?' Rainer's slim figure

was in the doorway. 'My uncle has a little business to
attend to with Mr Grisben, and we don't dine for half
an hour. Shall I fetch you, or can you find your way
down? Come straight to the dining-room—the second
door on the left of the long gallery.'

He disappeared, leaving a ray of warmth behind
him, and Faxon, relieved, lit a cigarette and sat down
by the fire.

Looking about with less haste, he was struck by a
detail that had escaped him. The room was full of
flowers—a mere 'bachelor's room', in the wing of a
house opened only for a few days, in the dead middle
of a New Hampshire winter! Flowers were everywhere,
not in senseless profusion, but placed with the same
conscious art that he had remarked in the grouping of
the blossoming shrubs in the hall. A vase of arums
stood on the writing table, a cluster of strange-hued
carnations on the stand at his elbow, and from bowls
of glass and porcelain clumps of freesia-bulbs diffused
their melting fragrance. The fact implied acres of
glass—but that was the least interesting part of it.
The flowers themselves, their quality, selection and
arrangement, attested on someone's part—and on
whose but John Lavington's?—a solicitous and sensi-
tive passion for that particular form of beauty. Well it
simply made the man, as he had appeared to Faxon,
all the harder to understand!

The half-hour elapsed, and Faxon, rejoicing at
the prospect of food, set out to make his way to the
dining-room. He had not noticed the direction he had
followed in going to his room, and was puzzled, when
he left it, to find that two staircases, of apparently
equal importance, invited him. He chose the one to his
right, and reached, at its foot, a long gallery such as
Rainer had described. The gallery was empty, the
doors down its length were closed; but Rainer had

said: 'The second to the left,' and Faxon, after pausing for some chance enlightenment which did not come, laid his hand on the second knob to the left.

The room he entered was square, with dusky picture-hung walls. In its centre, about a table lit with veiled lamps, he fancied Mr Lavington and his guests to be already seated at dinner; then he perceived that the table was covered not with viands but with papers, and that he had blundered into what seemed to be his host's study. As he paused Frank Rainer looked up.

'Oh, here's Mr Faxon. Why not ask him—?'

Mr Lavington, from the end of the table, reflected his nephew's smile in a glance of impartial benevolence.

'Certainly. Come in, Mr Faxon, if you won't think it a liberty—'

Mr Grisben, who sat opposite his host, turned his head toward the door. 'Of course Mr Faxon's an American citizen?'

Frank Rainer laughed. 'That's all right! … Oh, no, not one of your pin-pointed pens, Uncle Jack! Haven't you got a quill somewhere?'

Mr Balch, who spoke slowly and as if reluctantly, in a muffled voice of which there seemed to be very little left, raised his hand to say: 'One moment: you acknowledge this to be—?'

'My last will and testament?' Rainer's laugh redoubled. 'Well, I won't answer for the 'last'. It's the first, anyway.'

'It's mere formula,' Mr Balch explained.

'Well here goes.' Rainer dipped his quill in the inkstand his uncle had pushed in his direction, and dashed a gallant signature across the document.

Faxon, understanding what was expected of him, and conjecturing that the young man was signing his will on the attainment of his majority, had placed him-

self behind Mr Grisben, and stood awaiting his turn
to affix his name to the instrument. Rainer, having
signed, was about to push the paper across the table to
Mr Balch; but the latter, again raising his hand, said in
his sad imprisoned voice: 'The seal—?'

'Oh, does there have to be a seal?'

Faxon, looking over Mr Grisben at John Lavington,
saw a faint frown between his impassive eyes. 'Really,
Frank!' He seemed, Faxon thought, slightly irritated
by his nephew's frivolity.

'Who's got a seal?' Frank Rainer continued, glanc-
ing about the table. 'There doesn't seem to be one
here.'

Mr Grisben interposed. 'A wafer will do. Lavington,
you have a wafer?'

Mr Lavington had recovered his serenity. 'There
must be some in one of the drawers. But I'm ashamed
to say I don't know where my secretary keeps these
things. He ought to have seen to it that a wafer was
sent with the document.'

'Oh, hang it—' Frank Rainer pushed the paper
aside: 'It's the hand of God—and I'm as hungry as a
wolf. Let's dine first, Uncle Jack.'

'I think I've got a seal upstairs,' said Faxon.

Mr Lavington sent him a barely perceptible smile.

'So sorry to give you the trouble—'

'Oh, I say, don't send him after it now. Let's wait till
after dinner!'

Mr Lavington continued to smile on his guest, and
the latter, as if under the faint coercion of the smile,
turned from the room and ran upstairs. Having taken
the seal from his writing case he came down again, and
once more opened the door of the study. No one was
speaking when he entered—they were evidently awaiting his return with the mute impatience of hunger, and
he put the seal in Rainer's reach, and stood watching

while Mr Grisben struck a match and held it to one of the candles flanking the inkstand. As the wax descended on the paper Faxon remarked again the strange emaciation, the premature physical weariness, of the hand that held it: he wondered if Mr Lavington had ever noticed his nephew's hand, and if it were not poignantly visible to him now.

With this thought in his mind, Faxon raised his eyes to look at Mr Lavington. The great man's gaze rested on Frank Rainer with an expression of untroubled benevolence; and at the same instant Faxon's attention was attracted by the presence in the room of another person, who must have joined the group while he was upstairs searching for the seal. The new-comer was a man of about Mr Lavington's age and figure, who stood just behind his chair, and who, at the moment when Faxon first saw him, was gazing at young Rainer with an equal intensity of attention. The likeness of the two men—perhaps increased by the fact that the hooded lamps on the table left the figure behind the chair in shadow—struck Faxon the more because of the contrast in their expression. John Lavington, during his nephew's clumsy attempt to drop the wax and apply the seal, continued to fasten on him a look of half-amused affection; while the man behind the chair, so oddly reduplicating the lines of his features and figure, turned on the boy a face of pale hostility.

The impression was so startling that Faxon forgot what was going on about him. He was just dimly aware of young Rainer exclaiming: 'Your turn, Mr Grisben!' of Mr Grisben protesting: 'No—no; Mr Faxon first,' and of the pen being thereupon transferred to his own hand. He received it with a deadly sense of being unable to move, or even to understand what was expected of him, till he became conscious of Mr Grisben paternally pointing out the precise spot on which he was to leave his autograph. The effort to fix his attention and steady his hand prolonged the process of signing, and when he stood up—a strange weight of fatigue on all his limbs—the figure behind Mr Lavington's chair was gone.

Faxon felt an immediate sense of relief. It was puzzling that the man's exit should have been so rapid and noiseless, but the door behind Mr Lavington was screened by a tapestry hanging, and Faxon concluded that the unknown looker-on had merely had to raise it to pass out. At any rate he was gone, and with his withdrawal the strange weight was lifted. Young Rainer was lighting a cigarette, Mr Balch inscribing his name at the foot of the document, Mr Lavington—his eyes no longer on his nephew—examining a strange white-winged orchid in the vase at his elbow. Everything suddenly seemed to have grown natural and simple again, and Faxon found himself responding with a smile to the affable gesture with which his host declared: 'And now, Mr Faxon, we'll dine.'

III

'I wonder how I blundered into the wrong room just now; I thought you told me to take the second door to the left,' Faxon said to Frank Rainer as they followed the older men down the gallery.

'So I did; but I probably forgot to tell you which staircase to take. Coming from your bedroom, I ought to have said the fourth door to the right. It's a puzzling house because my uncle keeps adding to it from year to year. He built this room last summer for his modern pictures.' Young Rainer, pausing to open another door, touched an electric button which sent a circle of

light about the walls of a long room hung with can-
vases of the French Impressionist school.

Faxon, advanced, attracted by a shimmering Monet,
but Rainer laid a hand on his arm.

'He bought that last week. But come along—I'll
show you all this after dinner. Or *he* will, rather—he
loves it.'

'Does he really love things?'

Rainer stared, clearly perplexed at the question.
'Rather! Flowers and pictures especially! Haven't you
noticed the flowers? I suppose you think his manner's
cold; it seems so at first; but he's really awfully keen
about things.'

Faxon looked quickly at the speaker. 'Has your
uncle a brother?'

'Brother? No—never had. He and my mother were
the only ones.'

'Or any relation who—who looks like him? Who
might be mistaken for him?'

'Not that I ever heard of. Does he remind you of
someone?'

'Yes.'

'That's queer. We'll ask him if he's got a double.
Come on!'

But another picture had arrested Faxon, and some
minutes elapsed before he and his young host reached
the dining-room. It was a large room, with the same
conventionally handsome furniture and delicately
grouped flowers; and Faxon's first glance showed him
that only three men were seated about the dining-table.
The man who had stood behind Mr Lavington's chair
was not present, and no seat awaited him.

When the young men entered, Mr Grisben was
speaking, and his host, who faced the door, sat looking
down at his untouched soup-plate and turning the
spoon about in his small dry hand.

'It's pretty late to call them rumours—they were devilish close to facts when we left town this morning,' Mr Grisben was saying, with an unexpected incisiveness of tone.

Mr Lavington laid down his spoon and smiled interrogatively. 'Oh facts—what *are* facts? Just the way a thing happens to look at a given minute ...'

'You haven't heard anything from town?' Mr Grisben persisted.

'Not a syllable. So you see ... Balch, a little more of that *petite marmite*. Mr Faxon ... between Frank and Mr Grisben, please.'

The dinner progressed through a series of complicated courses, ceremoniously dispensed by a prelatical butler attended by three tall footmen, and it was evident that Mr Lavington took a certain satisfaction in the pageant. That, Faxon reflected, was probably the joint in his armour—that and the flowers. He had changed the subject—not abruptly but firmly—when the young men entered, but Faxon perceived that it still possessed the thoughts of the two elderly visitors, and Mr Balch presently observed, in a voice that seemed to come from the last survivor down a mineshaft: 'If it *does* come, it will be the biggest crash since '93.'

Mr Lavington looked bored but polite. 'Wall Street can stand crashes better than it could then. It's got a robuster constitution.'

'Yes; but—'

'Speaking of constitutions,' Mr Grisben intervened: 'Frank, are you taking care of yourself?'

A flush rose to young Rainer's cheeks.

'Why of course! Isn't that what I'm here for?'

'You're here about three days in the month, aren't you? And the rest of the time it's crowded restaurants and hot ballrooms in town. I thought you were to be shipped off to New Mexico?'

'Oh, I've got a new man who says that's rot.'

'Well, you don't look as if your new man were right,' said Mr Grisben bluntly.

Faxon saw the lad's colour fade, and the rings of shadow deepen under his gay eyes. At the same moment his uncle turned to him with a renewed intensity of attention. There was such solicitude in Mr Lavington's gaze that it seemed almost to fling a shield between his nephew and Mr Grisben's tactless scrutiny.

'We think Frank's a good deal better,' he began; 'this new doctor—'

The butler, coming up, bent to whisper a word in his ear, and the communication caused a sudden change in Mr Lavington's expression. His face was naturally so colourless that it seemed not so much to pale as to fade, to dwindle and recede into something blurred and blotted-out. He half rose, sat down again and sent a rigid smile about the table.

'Will you excuse me? The telephone. Peters, go on with the dinner.' With small precise steps he walked out of the door which one of the footmen had thrown open.

A momentary silence fell on the group; then Mr Grisben once more addressed himself to Rainer. 'You ought to have gone, my boy; you ought to have gone.'

The anxious look returned to the youth's eyes. 'My uncle doesn't think so, really.'

'You're not a baby, to be always governed by your uncle's opinion. You came of age to-day, didn't you? Your uncle spoils you ... that's what's the matter ...'

The thrust evidently went home, for Rainer laughed and looked down with a slight accession of colour.

'But the doctor—'

'Use your common sense, Frank! You had to try twenty doctors to find one to tell you what you wanted to be told.'

A look of apprehension overshadowed Rainer's gaiety.

'Oh, come—I say! ... What would you do?' he stammered.

'Pack up and jump on the first train.' Mr Grisben leaned forward and laid his hand kindly on the young man's arm. 'Look here: my nephew Jim Grisben is out there ranching on a big scale. He'll take you in and be glad to have you. You say your new doctor thinks it won't do you any good; but he doesn't pretend to say it will do you harm, does he? Well, then—give it a trial. It'll take you out of hot theatres and night restaurants, anyhow ... And all the rest of it ... Eh, Balch?'

'Go!' said Mr Balch hollowly. 'Go *at once*,' he added, as if a closer look at the youth's face had impressed on him the need of backing up his friend.

Young Rainer had turned ashy-pale. He tried to stiffen his mouth into a smile. 'Do I look as bad as all that?'

Mr Grisben was helping himself to terrapin. 'You look like the day after an earthquake,' he said.

The terrapin had encircled the table, and been deliberately enjoyed by Mr Lavington's three visitors (Rainer, Faxon noticed, left his plate untouched) before the door was thrown open to re-admit their host.

Mr Lavington advanced with an air of recovered composure. He seated himself, picked up his napkin and consulted the gold-monogrammed menu. 'No, don't bring back the filet ... Some terrapin; yes ...' He looked affably about the table. 'Sorry to have deserted you, but the storm has played the deuce with the wires, and I had to wait a long time before I could get a good connection. It must be blowing up for a blizzard.'

'Uncle Jack,' young Rainer broke out, 'Mr Grisben's been lecturing me.'

Mr Lavington was helping himself to terrapin. 'Ah—what about?'

'He thinks I ought to have given New Mexico a show.'

'I want him to go straight out to my nephew at Santa Paz and stay there till his next birthday.'

Mr Lavington signed to the butler to hand the terrapin to Mr Grisben, who, as he took a second helping, addressed himself again to Rainer. 'Jim's in New York now, and going back the day after tomorrow in Olyphant's private car. I'll ask Olyphant to squeeze you in if you'll go. And when you've been out there a week or two, in the saddle all day and sleeping nine hours a night, I suspect you won't think much of the doctor who prescribed New York.'

Faxon spoke up, he knew not why. 'I was out there once: it's a splendid life. I saw a fellow—oh, a really *bad* case—who'd been simply made over by it.'

'It *does* sound jolly,' Rainer laughed, a sudden eagerness in his tone.

His uncle looked at him gently. 'Perhaps Grisben's right. It's an opportunity—'

Faxon glanced up with a start: the figure dimly perceived in the study was now more visibly and tangibly planted behind Mr Lavington's chair.

'That's right, Frank: you see your uncle approves. And the trip out there with Olyphant isn't a thing to be missed. So drop a few dozen dinners and be at the Grand Central the day after tomorrow at five.'

Mr Grisben's pleasant grey eye sought corroboration of his host, and Faxon, in a cold anguish of suspense, continued to watch him as he turned his glance on Mr Lavington. One could not look at Lavington without seeing the presence at his back, and it was clear that, the next minute, some change in Mr Grisben's expression must give his watcher a clue.

But Mr Grisben's expression did not change: the gaze he fixed on his host remained unperturbed, and the clue he gave was the startling one of not seeming to see the other figure.

Faxon's first impulse was to look away, to look anywhere else, to resort again to the champagne glass the watchful butler had already brimmed; but some fatal attraction, at war in him with an overwhelming physical resistance, held his eyes upon the spot they feared.

The figure was still standing, more distinctly, and therefore more resemblingly, at Mr Lavington's back; and while the latter continued to gaze affectionately at his nephew, his counterpart, as before, fixed young Rainer with eyes of deadly menace.

Faxon, with what felt like an actual wrench of the muscles, dragged his own eyes from the sight to scan the other countenances about the table; but not one revealed the least consciousness of what he saw, and a sense of mortal isolation sank upon him.

'It's worth considering, certainly—' he heard Mr Lavington continue; and as Rainer's face lit up, the face behind his uncle's chair seemed to gather into its look all the fierce weariness of old unsatisfied hates. That was the thing that, as the minutes laboured by, Faxon was becoming most conscious of. The watcher behind the chair was no long merely malevolent: he had grown suddenly, unutterably tired. His hatred seemed to well up out of the very depths of balked effort and thwarted hopes, and the fact made him more pitiable, and yet more dire.

Faxon's look reverted to Mr Lavington, as if to surprise in him a corresponding change. At first none was visible: his pinched smile was screwed to his blank face like a gas-light to a white-washed wall. Then the fixity of the smile became ominous: Faxon saw that its wearer was afraid to let it go. It was evident that Mr Lavington was unutterably tired too, and the discovery sent a colder current through Faxon's veins. Looking down at his untouched plate, he caught the soliciting twinkle of the champagne glass; but the sight of the wine turned him sick.

'Well, we'll go into the details presently,' he heard Mr Lavington say, still on the question of his nephew's future. 'Let's have a cigar first. No—not here, Peters.' He turned his smile on Faxon. 'When we've had coffee I want to show you my pictures.'

'Oh, by the way, Uncle Jack—Mr Faxon wants to know if you've got a double?'

'A double?' Mr Lavington, still smiling, continued to address himself to his guest. 'Not that I know of. Have you seen one, Mr Faxon?'

Faxon thought: 'My God, if I look up now they'll both be looking at me!' To avoid raising his eyes he made as though to lift the glass to his lips; but his hand sank inert, and he looked up. Mr Lavington's glance was politely bent on him, but with a loosening of the strain about his heart he saw that the figure behind the chair still kept its gaze on Rainer.

'Do you think you've seen my double, Mr Faxon?'

Would the other face turn if he said yes? Faxon felt a dryness in his throat. 'No,' he answered.

'Ah? It's possible I've a dozen. I believe I'm extremely usual-looking.' Mr Lavington went on conversationally; and still the other face watched Rainer.

'It was … a mistake … a confusion of memory …' Faxon heard himself stammer. Mr Lavington pushed back his chair, and as he did so Mr Grisben suddenly leaned forward.

'Lavington! What have we been thinking of? We haven't drunk Frank's health!'

Mr Lavington reseated himself. 'My dear boy! ... Peters, another bottle ... ' He turned to his nephew.

'After such a sin of omission I don't presume to propose the toast myself ... but Frank knows ... Go ahead, Grisben!'

The boy shone on his uncle. 'No, no, Uncle Jack! Mr Grisben won't mind. Nobody but *you*—today!'

The butler was replenishing the glasses. He filled Mr Lavington's last, and Mr Lavington put out his small hand to raise it ... As he did so, Faxon looked away.

"Well, then—All the good I've wished you in all the past years ... I put it into the prayer that the coming ones may be healthy and happy and many ... and *many*, dear boy!'

Faxon saw the hands about him reach out for their glasses. Automatically, he reached for his. His eyes were still on the table, and he repeated to himself with a trembling vehemence: 'I won't look up! I won't ... I won't ...'

His fingers clasped the glass and raised it to the level of his lips. He saw the other hands making the same motion. He heard Mr Grisben's genial 'Hear! Hear!' and Mr Balch's hollow echo.

He said to himself as the rim of the glass touched his lips: 'I won't look up! I swear I won't—' and he looked.

The glass was so full that it required an extraordinary effort to hold it there, brimming and suspended, during the awful interval before he could trust his hand to lower it again, untouched, to the table. It was this merciful preoccupation which saved him, kept him from crying out, from losing his hold, from slipping down into the bottomless blackness that gaped for him. As long as the problem of the glass engaged him he felt able to keep his seat, manage his muscles, fit unnoticeably into the group; but as the glass touched

the table his last link with safety snapped. He stood up
and dashed out of the room.

IV

In the gallery, the instinct of self-preservation helped
him to turn back and sign to young Rainer not to
follow. He stammered out something about a touch
of dizziness, and joining them presently; and the boy
nodded sympathetically and drew back.

At the foot of the stairs Faxon ran against a servant.
'I should like to telephone to Weymore,' he said with
dry lips.

'Sorry, sir; wires all down. We've been trying the
last hour to get New York again for Mr Lavington.'

Faxon shot on to his room, burst into it, and bolted
the door. The lamplight lay on furniture, flowers,
books; in the ashes a log still glimmered. He dropped
down on the sofa and hid his face. The room was pro-
foundly silent, the whole house was still: nothing about
him gave a hint of what was going on, darkly and
dumbly, in the room he had flown from, and with the
covering of his eyes oblivion and reassurance seemed
to fall on him. But they fell for a moment only; then
his lids opened again to the monstrous vision. There it
was, stamped on his pupils, a part of him forever, an
indelible horror burnt into his body and brain. But
why into his—just his? Why had he alone been chosen
to see what he had seen? What business was it of *his*,
in God's name? Any one of the others, thus enlight-
ened, might have exposed the horror and defeated it;
but *he*, the one weaponless and defenceless spectator,
the one whom none of the others would believe or
understand if he attempted to reveal what he knew—

he alone had been singled out as the victim of this
dreadful initiation!

Suddenly he sat up, listening: he had heard a step on
the stairs. Someone, no doubt, was coming to see how
he was—to urge him, if he felt better, to go down and
join the smokers. Cautiously he opened the door; yes,
it was young Rainer's step. Faxon looked down the
passage, remembered the other stairway and darted to
it. All he wanted was to get out of the house. Not
another instant would he breathe its abominable air!
What business was it of *his*, in God's name?

He reached the opposite end of the lower gallery and
beyond it saw the hall by which he had entered. It was
empty, and on a long table he recognised his coat and
cap. He got into his coat, unbolted the door, and
plunged into the purifying night.

The darkness was deep, and the cold so intense that
for an instant it stopped his breathing. Then he perceived that only a thin snow was falling, and resolutely
he set his face for flight. The trees along the avenue
marked his way as he hastened with long strides over
the beaten snow. Gradually, while he walked, the
tumult in his brain subsided. The impulse to fly still
drove him forward, but he began to feel that he was
flying from a terror of his own creating, and that the
most urgent reason for escape was the need of hiding
his state, of shunning other eyes till he should regain
his balance.

He had spent the long hours in the train in fruitless
broodings on a discouraging situation, and he remembered how his bitterness had turned to exasperation
when he found that the Weymore sleigh was not awaiting him. It was absurd, of course; but, though he had
joked with Rainer over Mrs Culme's forgetfulness, to
confess it had cost a pang. That was what his rootless
life had brought him to; for lack of a personal stake in

things his sensibility was at the mercy of such trifles ...
Yes; that, and the cold and fatigue, the absence of hope
and the haunting sense of starved aptitudes, all these
had brought him to the perilous verge over which,
once or twice before, his terrified brain had hung.

Why else, in the name of any imaginable logic,
human or devilish, should he, a stranger, be singled
out for this experience? What could it mean to him,
how was he related to it, what bearing had it on his
case? ... Unless, indeed, it was just because he was a
stranger—a stranger everywhere—because he had no
personal life, no warm screen of private egotisms to
shield him from exposure, that he had developed this
abnormal sensitiveness to the vicissitudes of others.
The thought pulled him up with a shudder. No! Such a
fate was too abominable; all that was strong and sound
in him rejected it. A thousand times better regard himself as ill, disorganised, deluded, than as the predestined victim of such warnings!

He reached the gates and paused before the dark-
ened lodge. The wind had risen and was sweeping the
snow into his face. The cold had him in its grasp again,
and he stood uncertain. Should he put his sanity to the
test and go back? He turned and looked down the
dark drive to the house. A single ray shone through
the trees, evoking a picture of the lights, the flowers,
the faces grouped about that fatal room. He turned
and plunged out into the road ...

He remembered that, about a mile from Overdale,
the coachman had pointed out the road to Northridge;
and he began to walk in that direction. Once in the
road he had the gale in his face, and the wet snow on
his moustache and eye-lashes instantly hardened to ice.
The same ice seemed to be driving a million blades
into his throat and lungs, but he pushed on, the vision
of the warm room pursuing him.

The snow in the road was deep and uneven. He stumbled across ruts and sank into drifts, and the wind drove against him like a granite cliff. Now and then he stopped, gasping, as if an invisible hand had tightened an iron band about his body; then he started again, stiffening himself against the stealthy penetration of the cold. The snow continued to descend out of a pall of inscrutable darkness, and once or twice he paused, fearing he had missed the road to Northridge; but, seeing no sign of a turn, he ploughed on.

At last, feeling sure that he had walked for more than a mile, he halted and looked back. The act of turning brought immediate relief, first because it put his back to the wind, and then because, far down the road, it showed him the gleam of a lantern. A sleigh was coming—a sleigh that might perhaps give him a lift to the village! Fortified by the hope, he began to walk back toward the light. It came forward very slowly, with unaccountable zigzags and waverings; and even when he was within a few yards of it he could catch no sound of sleigh-bells. Then it paused and became stationary by the roadside, as though carried by a pedestrian who had stopped, exhausted by the cold. The thought made Faxon hasten on, and a moment later he was stooping over a motionless figure huddled against the snow-bank. The lantern had dropped from its bearer's hand, and Faxon, fearfully raising it, threw its light into the face of Frank Rainer.

'Rainer! What on earth are you doing here?'

The boy smiled back through his pallor. 'What are *you*, I'd like to know?' he retorted; and, scrambling to his feet with a clutch on Faxon's arm, he added gaily: 'Well, I've run you down!'

Faxon stood confounded, his heart sinking. The lad's face was grey.

'What madness—' he began.

'Yes, it *is*. What on earth did you do it for?'

'I? Do what? …. Why I …. I was just taking a walk
… I often walk at night …'

Frank Rainer burst into a laugh. 'On such nights?
Then you hadn't bolted?'

'Bolted?'

'Because I'd done something to offend you? My
uncle thought you had.'

Faxon grasped his arm. 'Did your uncle send you
after me?'

'Well, he gave me an awful rowing for not going up
to your room with you when you said you were ill.
And when we found you'd gone we were frightened—
and he was awfully upset—so I said I'd catch you …
You're *not* ill, are you?'

'Ill? No. Never better.' Faxon picked up the lantern.
'Come; let's go back. It was awfully hot in that dining-
room.'

'Yes; I hoped it was only that.'

They trudged on in silence for a few minutes; then
Faxon questioned: 'You're not too done up?'

'Oh, no. It's a lot easier with the wind behind us.'

'All right. Don't talk any more.'

They pushed ahead, walking, in spite of the light
that guided them, more slowly than Faxon had walked
alone into the gale. The fact of his companion's stum-
bling against a drift gave Faxon a pretext for saying:
'Take hold of my arm,' and Rainer, obeying, gasped
out: 'I'm blown!'

'So am I. Who wouldn't be?'

'What a dance you led me! If it hadn't been for one
of the servants happening to see you—'

'Yes: all right. And now, won't you kindly shut up?'

Rainer laughed and hung on him. 'Oh, the cold
doesn't hurt me …'

For the first few minutes after Rainer had overtaken

him, anxiety for the lad had been Faxon's only
thought. But as each labouring step carried them
nearer to the spot he had been fleeing, the reasons for
his flight grew more ominous and more insistent. No,
he was not ill, he was not distraught and deluded—he
was the instrument singled out to warn and save; and
here he was, irresistibly driven, dragging the victim
back to his doom!

The intensity of the conviction had almost checked
his steps. But what could he do or say? At all costs he
must get Rainer out of the cold, into the house and
into his bed. After that he would act.

The snow-fall was thickening, and as they reached
a stretch of the road between open fields the wind took
them at an angle, lashing their faces with barbed
thongs. Rainer stopped to take breath, and Faxon felt
the heavier pressure of his arm.

'When we get to the lodge, can't we telephone to the
stable for a sleigh?'

'If they're not all asleep at the lodge.'

'Oh, I'll manage. Don't talk!' Faxon ordered; and
they plodded on …

At length the lantern ray showed ruts that curved
away from the road under tree-darkness.

Faxon's spirits rose. 'There's the gate! We'll be there
in five minutes.'

As he spoke he caught, above the boundary hedge,
the gleam of a light at the farther end of the dark
avenue. It was the same light that had shone on the
scene of which every detail was burnt into his brain;
and he felt again its overpowering reality. No—he
couldn't let the boy go back!

They were at the lodge at last, and Faxon was ham-
mering on the door. He said to himself: 'I'll get him
inside first, and make them give him a hot drink. Then
I'll see—I'll find an argument …'

There was no answer to his knocking, and after an
interval Rainer said: 'Look here—we'd better go on.'

'No!'

'I can, perfectly—'

'You shan't go to the house, I say!' Faxon redoubled
his blows, and at length steps sounded on the stairs.
Rainer was leaning against the lintel, and as the door
opened the light from the hall flashed on his pale face
and fixed eyes. Faxon caught him by the arm and drew
him in.

'It *was* cold out there,' he sighed: and then, abruptly,
as if invisible shears at a single stroke had cut every
muscle in his body, he swerved, drooped on Faxon's
arm, and seemed to sink into nothing at his feet.

The lodge-keeper and Faxon bent over him, and
somehow, between them, lifted him into the kitchen
and laid him on a sofa by the stove.

The lodge-keeper, stammering: 'I'll ring up the
house,' dashed out of the room. But Faxon heard the
words without heeding them: omens mattered nothing
now, beside this woe fulfilled. He knelt down to undo
the fur collar about Rainer's throat, and as he did so
he felt a warm moisture on his hands. He held them
up, and they were red …

V

The palms threaded their endless line along the
yellow river. The little steamer lay at the wharf, and
George Faxon, sitting in the verandah of the wooden
hotel, idly watched the coolies carrying the freight
across the gang-plank.

He had been looking at such scenes for two months.
Nearly five had elapsed since he had descended from

the train at Northridge and strained his eyes for the
sleigh that was to take him to Weymore: Weymore,
which he was never to behold! ... Part of the interval—the first part—was still a great grey blur. Even
now he could not be quite sure how he had got back to
Boston, reached the house of a cousin, and been thence
transferred to a quiet room looking out on snow under
bare trees. He looked out a long time at the same
scene, and finally one day a man he had known at
Harvard came to see him and invited him to go out on
a business trip to the Malay peninsula.

'You've had a bad shake-up, and it'll do you no end
of good to get away from things.'

When the doctor came the next day it turned out
that he knew of the plan and approved it. 'You ought
to be quiet for a year, Just loaf and look at the landscape,' he advised.

Faxon felt the first faint stirrings of curiosity.

'What's been the matter with me, anyway?'

'Well, over-work, I suppose. You must have been
bottling up for a bad breakdown before you started for
New Hampshire last December. And the shock of that
poor boy's death did the rest.'

Ah, yes—Rainer had died. He remembered ...

He started for the East, and gradually, by impercep-
tible degrees, life crept back into his weary bones and
leaden brain. His friend was patient and considerate,
and they travelled slowly and talked little. At first
Faxon had felt a great shrinking from whatever
touched on familiar things. He seldom looked at a
newspaper and he never opened a letter without a con-
traction of the heart. It was not that he had any special
cause for apprehension, but merely that a great trail of
darkness lay on everything. He had looked too deep
down into the abyss ... But little by little health and
energy returned to him, and with them the common

promptings of curiosity. He was beginning to wonder
how the world was going, and when, presently, the
hotel keeper told him there were no letters for him in
the steamer's mail-bag, he felt a distinct sense of disappointment. His friend had gone into the jungle on a
long excursion, and he was lonely, unoccupied and
wholesomely bored. He got up and strolled into the
stuffy reading-room.

There he found a game of dominoes, a mutilated pic-
ture-puzzle, some copies of *Zion's Herald* and a pile of
New York and London newspapers.

He began to glance through the papers, and was dis-
appointed to find they were less recent than he had
hoped. Evidently the last numbers had been carried off
by luckier travellers. He continued to turn them over,
picking out the American ones first. These, as it happened, were the oldest: they dated back to December
and January. To Faxon, however, they had all the
flavour of novelty, since they covered the precise
period during which he had virtually ceased to exist. It
had never before occurred to him to wonder what had
happened in the world during that interval of oblitera-
tion; but now he felt a sudden desire to know.

To prolong the pleasure, he began by sorting the
papers chronologically, and as he found and spread
out the earliest number, the date at the top of the page
entered into his consciousness like a key slipping into a
lock. It was the seventeenth of December: the date of
the day after his arrival at Northridge. He glanced at
the first page and read in blazing characters: *'Reported
Failure of Opal Cement Company. Lavington's Name
Involved. Gigantic Exposure of Corruption Shakes Wall
Street To Its Foundations.'*

He read on, and when he had finished the first paper
he turned to the next. There was a gap of three days,
but the Opal Cement 'Investigation' still held the centre

of the stage. From its complex revelations of greed and
ruin his eye wandered to the death notices, and he
read:

'Rainer. Suddenly, at Northridge, New Hampshire,
Frances John, only son of the late ...'

His eyes clouded, and he dropped the newspaper
and sat for a long time with his face in his hands.
When he looked up again he noticed that his gesture
had pushed the other papers from the table and scat-
tered them at his feet. The uppermost lay spread out
before him, and heavily his eyes began their search
again. *'John Lavington comes forward with plan for*
reconstructing Company. Offers to put in ten millions of
his own—The proposal under consideration by the
District Attorney.'

Ten millions ... ten millions of his own. But if John
Lavington was ruined? ... Faxon stood up with a cry.
That was it, then—that was what the warning meant!
And if he had not fled from it, dashed wildly away
from it into the night, he might have broken the spell
of iniquity, the powers of darkness might not have pre-
vailed! He caught up the pile of newspapers and began
to glance through each in turn for the head-line: 'Wills
Admitted to Probate.' In the last of all he found the
paragraph he sought, and it stared up at him as if with
Rainer's dying eyes.

That—*that* was what he had done! The powers of
pity had singled him out to warn and save, and he had
closed his ears to their call, and washed his hands of
it, and fled. Washed his hands of it! That was the
word. It caught him back to the dreadful moment in
the lodge when, raising himself up from Rainer's
side, he had looked at his hands and seen that they
were red ...

The Eyes

I

WE HAD BEEN PUT IN THE MOOD FOR GHOSTS, that evening, after an excellent dinner at our old friend Culwin's, by a tale of Fred Murchard's—the narrative of a strange personal visitation.

Seen through the haze of our cigars, and by the drowsy gleam of a coal fire, Culwin's library, with its oak walls and dark old bindings, made a good setting for such evocations; and ghostly experiences at first hand being, after Murchard's brilliant opening, the only kind acceptable to us, we proceeded to take stock of our group and tax each member for a contribution. There were eight of us, and seven contrived, in a manner more or less adequate, to fulfil the condition imposed. It surprised us all to find that we could muster such a show of supernatural impressions, for none of us, excepting Murchard himself and young Phil Frenham—whose story was the slightest of the lot—had the habit of sending our souls into the invisible. So that, on the whole, we had every reason to be proud of our seven 'exhibits', and none of us would have dreamed of expecting an eighth from our host.

Our old friend, Mr Andrew Culwin, who had sat back in his arm-chair, listening and blinking through the smoke circles with the cheerful tolerance of a wise old idol, was not the kind of man likely to be favoured with such contacts, though he had imagination enough to enjoy, without envying, the superior privileges of his guests. By age and by education he belonged to the stout Positivist tradition, and his habit of thought had been formed in the days of the epic struggle between

physics and metaphysics. But he had been, then and
always, essentially a spectator, a humorous detached
observer of the immense muddled variety show of life,
slipping out of his seat now and then for a brief dip
into the convivialities at the back of the house, but
never, as far as one knew, showing the least desire to
jump on the stage and do a 'turn'.

Among his contemporaries there lingered a vague
tradition of his having, at a remote period, and in a
romantic clime, been wounded in a duel; but this
legend no more tallied with what we younger men
knew of his character than my mother's assertion that
he had once been 'a charming little man with nice eyes'
corresponded to any possible reconstitution of his
physiognomy.

'He never can have looked like anything but a
bundle of sticks,' Murchard had once said of him. 'Or
a phosphorescent log, rather,' someone else amended;
and we recognised the happiness of this description of
his small squat trunk, with the red blink of the eyes in
a face like mottled bark. He had always been possessed
of a leisure which he had nursed and protected, instead
of squandering it in vain activities. His carefully
guarded hours had been devoted to the cultivation of a
fine intelligence and a few judiciously chosen habits;
and none of the disturbances common to human experience seemed to have crossed his sky. Nevertheless,
his dispassionate survey of the universe had not raised
his opinion of that costly experiment, and his study
of the human race seemed to have resulted in the con-
clusion that all men were superfluous, and women
necessary only because someone had to do the cook-
ing. On the importance of this point his convictions
were absolute, and gastronomy was the only science
which he revered as a dogma. It must be owned that
his little dinners were a strong argument in favour of

this view, besides being a reason—though not the main one—for the fidelity of his friends.

Mentally he exercised a hospitality less seductive but no less stimulating. His mind was like a forum, or some open meeting-place for the exchange of ideas: somewhat cold and draughty, but light, spacious and orderly—a kind of academic grove from which all the leaves had fallen. In this privileged area a dozen of us were wont to stretch our muscles and expand our lungs; and, as if to prolong as much as possible the tradition of what we felt to be a vanishing institution, one or two neophytes were now and then added to our band.

Young Phil Frenham was the last, and the most interesting, of these recruits, and a good example of Murchard's somewhat morbid assertion that our old friend 'liked 'em juicy'. It was indeed a fact that Culwin, for all his dryness, specially tasted the lyric qualities in youth. As he was far too good an Epicurean to nip the flowers of soul which he gathered for his garden, his friendship was not a disintegrating influence: on the contrary, it forced the young idea to robuster bloom. And in Phil Frenham he had a fine subject for experimentation. The boy was really intelligent, and the soundness of his nature was like the pure paste under a delicate glaze. Culwin had fished him out of a thick fog of family dullness, and pulled him up to a peak in Darien; and the adventure hadn't hurt him a bit. Indeed, the skill with which Culwin had contrived to stimulate his curiosities without robbing them of their young bloom of awe seemed to me a sufficient answer to Murchard's ogreish metaphor. There was nothing hectic in Frenham's efflorescence, and his old friend had not laid even a finger-tip on the sacred stupidities. One wanted no better proof of that than the fact that Frenham still reverenced them in Culwin.

'There's a side of him you fellows don't see. I believe
that story about the duel!' he declared; and it was of
the very essence of this belief that it should impel
him—just as our little party was dispersing—to turn
back to our host with the absurd demand: 'And now
you've got to tell us about *your* ghost!'

The outer door had closed on Murchard and the
others; only Frenham and I remained; and the vigilant
servant who presided over Culwin's destinies, having
brought a fresh supply of soda-water, had been laconi-
cally ordered to bed.

Culwin's sociability was a night-blooming flower,
and we knew that he expected the nucleus of his group
to tighten around him after midnight. But Frenham's
appeal seemed to disconcert him comically, and he
rose from the chair in which he had just reseated himself after his farewells in the hall.

'*My* ghost? Do you suppose I'm fool enough to go to
the expense of keeping one of my own, when there are
so many charming ones in my friends' closets?—Take
another cigar,' he said, revolving toward me with a
laugh.

Frenham laughed too, pulling up his slender height
before the chimney-piece as he turned to face his short
bristling friend.

'Oh,' he said, 'you'd never be content to share if you
met one you really liked.'

Culwin had dropped back into his armchair, his
shock head embedded in its habitual hollow, his little
eyes glimmering over a fresh cigar.

'Liked—*liked*? Good Lord!' he growled.

'Ah, you *have*, then!' Frenham pounced on him
in the same instant, with a side-glance of victory
at me; but Culwin cowered gnomelike among his
cushions, dissembling himself in a protective cloud
of smoke.

'What's the use of denying it? You've seen everything, so of course you've seen a ghost!' his young
friend persisted, talking intrepidly into the cloud.
'Or, if you haven't seen one, it's only because you've
seen two!'

The form of the challenge seemed to strike our
host. He shot his head out of the mist with a queer
tortoise-like motion he sometimes had, and blinked
approvingly at Frenham.

'That's it,' he flung at us on a shrill jerk of laughter;
'it's only because I've seen two!'

The words were so unexpected that they dropped
down and down into a deep silence, while we continued to stare at each other over Culwin's head, and
Culwin stared at his ghosts. At length Frenham,
without speaking, threw himself into the chair on the
other side of the hearth, and leaned forward with his
listening smile …

II

'Oh, of course they're not show ghosts—a collector
wouldn't think anything of them … Don't let me raise
your hopes … their one merit is their numerical
strength: the exceptional fact of their being *two*. But,
as against this, I'm bound to admit that at any moment
I could probably have exorcised them both by asking
my doctor for a prescription, or my oculist for a pair of
spectacles. Only, as I never could make up my mind
whether to go to the doctor or the oculist—whether I
was afflicted by an optical or a digestive delusion—I
left them to pursue their interesting double life, though
at times they made mine exceedingly uncomfortable …

Yes—uncomfortable; and you know how I hate to

be uncomfortable! But it was part of my stupid pride, when the thing began, not to admit that I could be disturbed by the trifling matter of seeing two—

And then I'd no reason, really, to suppose I was ill. As far as I knew I was simply bored—horribly bored. But it was part of my boredom—I remember—that I was feeling so uncommonly well, and didn't know how on earth to work off my surplus energy. I had come back from a long journey—down in South America and Mexico—and had settled down for the winter near New York, with an old aunt who had known Washington Irving and corresponded with N. P. Willis. She lived, not far from Irvington, in a damp Gothic villa, overhung by Norway spruces, and look-ing exactly like a memorial emblem done in hair. Her personal appearance was in keeping with this image, and her own hair—of which there was little left— might have been sacrificed to the manufacture of the emblem.

I had just reached the end of an agitated year, with considerable arrears to make up in money and emotion; and theoretically it seemed as though my aunt's mild hospitality would be as beneficial to my nerves as to my purse. But the deuce of it was that as soon as I felt myself safe and sheltered my energy began to revive; and how was I to work it off inside of a memorial emblem? I had, at that time, the agreeable illusion that sustained intellectual effort could engage a man's whole activity; and I decided to write a great book—I forget about what. My aunt, impressed by my plan, gave up to me her Gothic library, filled with classics in black cloth and daguerreotypes of faded celebrities; and I sat down at my desk to make myself a place among their number. And to facilitate my task she lent me a cousin to copy my manuscript.

The cousin was a nice girl, and I had an idea that a

nice girl was just what I needed to restore my faith in human nature, and principally in myself. She was neither beautiful nor intelligent—poor Alice Nowell!— but it interested me to see any woman content to be so uninteresting, and I wanted to find out the secret of her content. In doing this I handled it rather rashly, and put it out of joint—oh, just for a moment! There's no fatuity in telling you this, for the poor girl had never seen anyone but cousins …

Well, I was sorry for what I'd done, of course, and confoundedly bothered as to how I should put it straight. She was staying in the house, and one evening, after my aunt had gone to bed, she came down to the library to fetch a book she'd mislaid, like any artless heroine on the shelves behind us. She was pink-nosed and flustered, and it suddenly occurred to me that her hair, though it was fairly thick and pretty, would look exactly like my aunt's when she grew older. I was glad I had noticed this, for it made it easier for me to do what was right; and when I had found the book she hadn't lost I told her I was leaving for Europe that week.

Europe was terribly far off in those days, and Alice knew at once what I meant. She didn't take it in the least as I'd expected—it would have been easier if she had. She held her book very tight, and turned away a moment to wind up the lamp on my desk—it had a ground glass shade with vine leaves, and glass drops around the edge, I remember. Then she came back, held out her hand, and said: 'Good-bye.' And as she said it she looked straight at me and kissed me. I had never felt anything as fresh and shy and brave as her kiss. It was worse than any reproach, and it made me ashamed to deserve a reproach from her. I said to myself: 'I'll marry her, and when my aunt dies she'll leave us this house, and I'll sit here at the desk and go

on with my book; and Alice will sit over there with her
embroidery and look at me as she's looking now. And
life will go on like that for any number of years.' The
prospect frightened me a little, but at the time it didn't
frighten me as much as doing anything to hurt her;
and ten minutes later she had my seal ring on my
finger, and my promise that when I went abroad she
should go with me.

You'll wonder why I'm enlarging on this familiar
incident. It's because the evening on which it took
place was the very evening on which I first saw the
queer sight I've spoken of. Being at that time an ardent
believer in a necessary sequence between cause and
effect I naturally tried to trace some kind of link
between what had just happened to me in my aunt's
library, and what was to happen a few hours later on
the same night; and so the coincidence between the two
events always remained in my mind.

I went up to bed with rather a heavy heart, for I was
bowed under the weight of the first good action I had
ever consciously committed; and young as I was, I saw
the gravity of my situation. Don't imagine from this
that I had hitherto been an instrument of destruction. I
had been merely a harmless young man, who had followed his bent and declined all collaboration with
Providence. Now I had suddenly undertaken to pro-
mote the moral order of the world, and I felt a good
deal like the trustful spectator who has given his gold
watch to the conjurer, and doesn't know in what shape
he'll get it back when the trick is over … Still, a glow
of self-righteousness tempered my fears, and I said to
myself as I undressed that when I'd got used to being
good it probably wouldn't make me as nervous as it
did at the start. And by the time I was in bed, and had
blown out my candle, I felt that I really *was* getting
used to it, and that, as far as I'd got, it was not unlike

sinking down into one of my aunt's very softest wool
mattresses.

I closed my eyes on this image, and when I opened
them it must have been a good deal later, for my room
had grown cold, and the night was intensely still. I was
waked by the queer feeling we all know—the feeling
that there was something in the room that hadn't been
there when I fell asleep. I sat up and strained my eyes
into the darkness. The room was pitch black, and at
first I saw nothing; but gradually a vague glimmer at
the foot of the bed turned into two eyes staring back at
me. I couldn't see the face attached to them—on
account of the darkness, I imagined—but as I looked
the eyes grew more and more distinct: they gave out a
light of their own.

The sensation of being thus gazed at was far from
pleasant, and you might suppose that my first impulse
would have been to jump out of bed and hurl myself
on the invisible figure attached to the eyes. But it
wasn't—my impulse was simply to lie still … I can't
say whether this was due to an immediate sense of the
uncanny nature of the apparition—to the certainty
that if I did jump out of bed I should hurl myself on
nothing—or merely to the benumbing effect of the eyes
themselves. They were the very worst eyes I've ever
seen: a man's eyes—but what a man! My first thought
was that he must be frightfully old. The orbits were
sunk, and the thick red-lined lids hung over the eye-
balls like blinds of which the cords are broken. One lid
drooped a little lower than the other, with the effect of
a crooked leer; and between these folds of flesh, with
their scant bristle of lashes, the eyes themselves, small
glassy disks with an agate-like rim, looked like sea-
pebbles in the grip of a starfish.

But the age of the eyes was not the most unpleasant
thing about them. What turned me sick was their

expression of vicious security. I don't know how else to describe the fact that they seemed to belong to a man who had done a lot of harm in his life, but had always kept just inside the danger lines. They were not the eyes of a coward, but of someone much too clever to take risks; and my gorge rose at their look of base astuteness. Yet even that wasn't the worst; for as we continued to scan each other I saw in them a tinge of faint derision, and felt myself to be its object.

At that I was seized by an impulse of rage that jerked me to my feet and pitched me straight on the unseen figure. But of course there wasn't any figure there, and my fists struck at emptiness. Ashamed and cold, I groped about for a match and lit the candles. The room looked just as usual—as I had known it would; and I crawled back to bed, and blew out the lights.

As soon as the room was dark again the eyes reappeared; and I now applied myself to explaining them on scientific principles. At first I thought the illusion might have been caused by the glow of the last embers in the chimney; but the fire-place was on the other side of my bed, and so placed that the fire could not possibly be reflected in my toilet glass, which was the only mirror in the room. Then it struck me that I might have been tricked by the reflection of the embers in some polished bit of wood or metal; and though I couldn't discover any object of the sort in my line of vision, I got up again, groped my way to the hearth, and covered what was left of the fire. But as soon as I was back in bed the eyes were back at its foot.

They were an hallucination, then: that was plain. But the fact that they were not due to any external dupery didn't make them a bit pleasanter to see. For if they were a projection of my inner consciousness, what the deuce was the matter with that organ? I had gone deeply enough into the mystery of morbid pathological states to picture the conditions under which an exploring mind might lay itself open to such a midnight admonition; but I couldn't fit it to my present case. I had never felt more normal, mentally and physically; and the only unusual fact in my situation—that of having assured the happiness of an amiable girl—did not seem of a kind to summon unclean spirits about my pillow. But there were the eyes still looking at me ...

I shut mine, and tried to evoke a vision of Alice Nowell's. They were not remarkable eyes, but they were as wholesome as fresh water, and if she had had more imagination—or longer lashes—their expression might have been interesting. As it was, they did not prove very efficacious, and in a few moments I perceived that they had mysteriously changed into the eyes at the foot of the bed. It exasperated me more to feel these glaring at me through my shut lids than to see them, and I opened my eyes again and looked straight into their hateful stare ...

And so it went on all night. I can't tell you what that night was, nor how long it lasted. Have you ever lain in bed, hopelessly wide awake, and tried to keep your eyes shut, knowing that if you opened 'em you'd see something you dreaded and loathed? It sounds easy, but it's devilish hard. Those eyes hung there and drew me. I had the *vertige de l'abîme*, and their red lids were the edge of my abyss ... I had known nervous hours before: hours when I'd felt the wind of danger in my neck; but never this kind of strain. It wasn't that the eyes were so awful; they hadn't the majesty of the powers of darkness. But they had—how shall I say?—a physical effect that was the equivalent of a bad smell: their look left a smear like a snail's. And I didn't see what business they had with me, anyhow—and I stared and stared, trying to find out ...

I don't know what effect they were trying to produce; but the effect they *did* produce was that of making me pack my portmanteau and bolt to town early the next morning. I left a note for my aunt, explaining that I was ill and had gone to see my doctor; and as a matter of fact I did feel uncommonly ill—the night seemed to have pumped all the blood out of me. But when I reached town I didn't go to the doctor's. I went to a friend's rooms, and threw myself on a bed, and slept for ten heavenly hours. When I woke it was the middle of the night, and I turned cold at the thought of what might be waiting for me. I sat up, shaking, and stared into the darkness; but there wasn't a break in its blessed surface, and when I saw that the eyes were not there I dropped back into another long sleep.

I had left no word for Alice when I fled, because I meant to go back the next morning. But the next morning I was too exhausted to stir. As the day went on the exhaustion increased, instead of wearing off like the lassitude left by an ordinary night of insomnia: the effect of the eyes seemed to be cumulative, and the thought of seeing them again grew intolerable. For two days I fought my dread; but on the third evening I pulled myself together and decided to go back the next morning. I felt a good deal happier as soon as I'd decided, for I knew that my abrupt disappearance, and the strangeness of my not writing, must have been very painful for poor Alice. I went to bed with an easy mind, and fell asleep at once; but in the middle of the night I woke, and there were the eyes …

Well, I simply couldn't face them; and instead of going back to my aunt's I bundled a few things into a trunk and jumped on to the first steamer for England. I was so dead tired when I got on board that I crawled straight into my berth, and slept most of the way over; and I can't tell you the bliss it was to wake from those

long stretches of dreamless sleep and look fearlessly
into the darkness, knowing that I shouldn't see
the eyes ...

I stayed abroad for a year, and then I stayed for
another; and during that time I never had a glimpse
of them. That was enough reason for prolonging my
stay if I'd been on a desert island. Another was, of
course, that I had perfectly come to see, on the voyage
over, the complete impossibility of my marrying Alice
Nowell. The fact that I had been so slow in making
this discovery annoyed me, and made me want to
avoid explanations. The bliss of escaping at one stroke
from the eyes, and from this other embarrassment,
gave my freedom an extraordinary zest; and the longer
I savoured it the better I liked its taste.

The eyes had burned such a hole in my consciousness that for a long time I went on puzzling over the
nature of the apparition, and wondering if it would
ever come back. But as time passed I lost this dread,
and retained only the precision of the image. Then
that faded in its turn.

The second year found me settled in Rome, where I
was planning, I believe, to write another great book—
a definitive work on Etruscan influences in Italian art.
At any rate, I'd found some pretext of the kind for taking a sunny apartment in the Piazza di Spagna and
dabbling about in the Forum; and there, one morning,
a charming youth came to me. As he stood there in
the warm light, slender and smooth and hyacinthine,
he might have stepped from a ruined altar—one to
Antinous, say—but he'd come instead from New
York, with a letter (of all people) from Alice Nowell.
The letter—the first I'd had from her since our
break—was simply a line introducing her young
cousin, Gilbert Noyes, and appealing to me to
befriend him. It appeared, poor lad, that he 'had

talent', and 'wanted to write'; and, an obdurate family
having insisted that his calligraphy should take the
form of double entry, Alice had intervened to win him
six months' respite, during which he was to travel
abroad on a meagre pittance, and somehow prove his
ability to increase it by his pen. The quaint conditions
of the test struck me first: it seemed about as conclu-
sive as a mediæval 'ordeal'. Then I was touched by her
having sent him to me. I had always wanted to do her
some service, to justify myself in my own eyes rather
than hers; and here was a beautiful occasion.

I imagine it's safe to lay down the general principle
that predestined geniuses don't, as a rule, appear
before one in the spring sunshine of the Forum looking
like one of its banished gods. At any rate, poor Noyes
wasn't a predestined genius. But he *was* beautiful to
see, and charming as a comrade. It was only when he
began to talk literature that my heart failed me. I knew
all the symptoms so well—the things he had 'in him',
and the things outside him that impinged! There's the
real test, after all. It was always—punctually,
inevitably, with the inexorableness of a mechanical
law—it was *always* the wrong thing that struck him. I
grew to find a certain fascination in deciding in
advance exactly which wrong thing he'd select; and I
acquired an astonishing skill at the game …

The worst of it was that his *bêtise* wasn't of the too
obvious sort. Ladies who met him at picnics thought
him intellectual; and even at dinners he passed for
clever. I, who had him under the microscope, fancied
now and then that he might develop some kind of a
slim talent, something that he could make 'do' and
be happy on; and wasn't that, after all, what I was
concerned with? He was so charming—he continued
to be so charming—that he called forth all my charity
in support of this argument; and for the first few

months I really believed there was a chance for him …

Those months were delightful. Noyes was constantly with me, and the more I saw of him the better I liked him. His stupidity was a natural grace—it was as beautiful, really, as his eyelashes. And he was so gay, so affectionate, and so happy with me, that telling him the truth would have been about as pleasant as slitting the throat of some gentle animal. At first I used to wonder what had put into that radiant head the detestable delusion that it held a brain. Then I began to see that it was simply protective mimicry—an instinctive ruse to get away from family life and an office desk. Not that Gilbert didn't—dear lad!— believe in himself. There wasn't a trace of hypocrisy in his composition. He was sure that his 'call' was irresistible, while to me it was the saving grace of his situation that it *wasn't*, and that a little money, a little leisure, a little pleasure would have turned him into an inoffensive idler. Unluckily, however, there was no hope of money, and with the grim alternative of the office desk before him he couldn't postpone his attempt at literature. The stuff he turned out was deplorable, and I see now that I knew it from the first. Still, the absurdity of deciding a man's whole future on a first trial seemed to justify me in withholding my verdict, and perhaps even in encouraging him a little, on the ground that the human plant generally needs warmth to flower.

At any rate, I proceeded on that principle, and carried it to the point of getting his term of probation extended. When I left Rome he went with me, and we idled away a delicious summer between Capri and Venice. I said to myself: 'If he has anything in him, it will come out now' and it did. He was never more enchanting and enchanted. There were moments of our pilgrimage when beauty born of murmuring sound seemed actually to pass into his face—but only to issue forth in a shallow flood of the palest ink …

Well the time came to turn off the tap; and I knew there was no hand but mine to do it. We were back in Rome, and I had taken him to stay with me, not wanting him to be alone in his dismal *pension* when he had to face the necessity of renouncing his ambition. I hadn't, of course, relied solely on my own judgment in deciding to advise him to drop literature. I had sent his stuff to various people—editors and critics—and they had always sent it back with the same chilling lack of comment. Really there was nothing on earth to say—

I confess I never felt more shabbily than I did on the day when I decided to have it out with Gilbert. It was well enough to tell myself that it was my duty to knock the poor boy's hopes into splinters—but I'd like to know what act of gratuitous cruelty hasn't been justified on that plea? I've always shrunk from usurping the functions of Providence, and when I have to exercise them I decidedly prefer that it shouldn't be on an errand of destruction. Besides, in the last issue, who was I to decide, even after a year's trial, if poor Gilbert had it in him or not?

The more I looked at the part I'd resolved to play, the less I liked it; and I liked it still less when Gilbert sat opposite me, with his head thrown back in the lamplight, just as Phil's is now … I'd been going over his last manuscript, and he knew it, and he knew that his future hung on my verdict—we'd tacitly agreed to that. The manuscript lay between us, on my table—a novel, his first novel, if you please!—and he reached over and laid his hand on it, and looked up at me with all his life in the look.

I stood up and cleared my throat, trying to keep my eyes away from his face and on the manuscript.

'The fact is, my dear Gilbert,' I began—

I saw him turn pale, but he was up and facing me an instant.

'Oh, look here, don't take on so, my dear fellow! I'm not so awfully cut up as all that!' His hands were on my shoulders, and he was laughing down on me from his full height, with a kind of mortally-stricken gaiety that drove the knife into my side.

He was too beautifully brave for me to keep up any humbug about my duty. And it came over me suddenly how I should hurt others in hurting him: myself first, since sending him home meant losing him; but more particularly poor Alice Nowell, to whom I had so longed to prove my good faith and my desire to serve her. It really seemed like failing her twice to fail Gilbert—

But my intuition was like one of those lightning flashes that encircle the whole horizon, and in the same instant I saw what I might be letting myself in for if I didn't tell the truth. I said to myself: 'I shall have him for life'—and I'd never yet seen anyone, man or woman, whom I was quite sure of wanting on those terms. Well, this impulse of egotism decided me. I was ashamed of it, and to get away from it I took a leap that landed me straight in Gilbert's arms.

'The thing's all right, and you're all wrong!' I shouted up at him; and as he hugged me, and I laughed and shook in his clutch, I had for a minute the sense of self-complacency that is supposed to attend the footsteps of the just. Hang it all, making people happy has its charms—

Gilbert, of course, was for celebrating his emancipation in some spectacular manner; but I sent him away alone to explode his emotions, and went to bed to sleep off mine. As I undressed I began to wonder what their after-taste would be—so many of the finest don't keep! Still, I wasn't sorry, and I meant to empty the bottle, even if it *did* turn a trifle flat.

After I got into bed I lay for a long time smiling at the memory of his eyes—his blissful eyes …Then I fell asleep, and when I woke the room was deathly cold, and I sat up with a jerk—and there were *the other eyes* …

It was three years since I'd seen them, but I'd thought of them so often that I fancied they could never take me unawares again. Now, with their red sneer on me, I knew that I had never really believed they would come back, and that I was as defenceless as ever against them … As before, it was the insane irrelevance of their coming that made it so horrible. What the deuce were they after, to leap out at me at such a time? I had lived more or less carelessly in the years since I'd seen them, though my worst indiscretions were not dark enough to invite the searchings of their infernal glare; but at this particular moment I was really in what might have been called a state of grace; and I can't tell you how the fact added to their horror…

But it's not enough to say they were as bad as before: they were worse. Worse by just so much as I'd learned of life in the interval; by all the damnable implications my wider experience read into them. I saw now what I hadn't seen before: that they were eyes which had grown hideous gradually, which had built up their baseness coral-wise, bit by bit, out of a series of small turpitudes slowly accumulated through the industrious years. Yes—it came to me that what made them so bad was that they'd grown bad so slowly …

There they hung in the darkness, their swollen lids dropped across the little watery bulbs rolling loose in the orbits, and the puff of fat flesh making a muddy shadow underneath—and as their stare moved with

my movements, there came over me a sense of their
tacit complicity, of a deep hidden understanding
between us that was worse than the first shock of their
strangeness. Not that I understood them; but that they
made it so clear that some day I should …Yes, that
was the worst part of it, decidedly; and it was the
feeling that became stronger each time they came back
to me …

For they got into the damnable habit of coming
back. They reminded me of vampires with a taste for
young flesh, they seemed so to gloat over the taste of
a good conscience. Every night for a month they came
to claim their morsel of mine: since I'd made Gilbert
happy they simply wouldn't loosen their fangs. The
coincidence almost made me hate him, poor lad, fortu-
itous as I felt it to be. I puzzled over it a good deal, but
couldn't find any hint of an explanation except in the
chance of his association with Alice Nowell. But then
the eyes had let up on me the moment I had abandoned her, so they could hardly be the emissaries of a
woman scorned, even if one could have pictured poor
Alice charging such spirits to avenge her. That set me
thinking, and I began to wonder if they would let up
on me if I abandoned Gilbert. The temptation was
insidious, and I had to stiffen myself against it; but
really, dear boy! he was too charming to be sacrificed
to such demons. And so, after all, I never found out
what they wanted …'

III

The fire crumbled, sending up a flash which threw into
relief the narrator's gnarled face under its grey-black
stubble. Pressed into the hollow of the chair back, it

stood out an instant like an intaglio of yellowish red-veined stone, with spots of enamel for the eyes; then the fire sank and in the shaded lamp-light it became once more a dim Rembrandtish blur.

Phil Frenham, sitting in a low chair on the opposite side of the hearth, one long arm propped on the table behind him, one hand supporting his thrown-back head, and his eyes steadily fixed on his old friend's face, had not moved since the tale began. He continued to maintain his silent immobility after Culwin had ceased to speak, and it was I who, with a vague sense of disappointment at the sudden drop of the story, finally asked: 'But how long did you keep on seeing them?'

Culwin, so sunk into his chair that he seemed like a heap of his own empty clothes, stirred a little, as if in surprise at my question. He appeared to have half-forgotten what he had been telling us.

'How long? Oh, off and on all that winter. It was infernal. I never got used to them. I grew really ill.'

Frenham shifted his attitude silently, and as he did so his elbow struck against a small mirror in a bronze frame standing on the table behind him. He turned and changed its angle slightly; then he resumed his former attitude, his dark head thrown back on his lifted palm, his eyes intent on Culwin's face.

Something in his stare embarrassed me, and as if to divert attention from it I pressed on with another question:

'And you never tried sacrificing Noyes?'

'Oh, no. The fact is I didn't have to. He did it for me, poor boy!'

'Did it for you? How do you mean?'

'He wore me out—wore everybody out. He kept on pouring out his lamentable twaddle, and hawking it up and down the place till he became a thing of terror. I

tried to wean him from writing—oh, ever so gently,
you understand, by throwing him with agreeable
people, giving him a chance to make himself felt, to
come to a sense of what he *really* had to give. I'd
foreseen this solution from the beginning—felt sure
that, once the first ardour of authorship was quenched,
he'd drop into his place as a charming parasitic thing,
the kind of chronic Cherubino for whom, in old soci-
eties, there's always a seat at table, and a shelter
behind the ladies' skirts. I saw him take his place as
'the poet': the poet who doesn't write. One knows the
type in every drawing-room. Living in that way doesn't
cost much—I'd worked it all out in my mind, and felt
sure that, with a little help, he could manage it for the
next few years; and meanwhile he'd be sure to marry. I
saw him married to a widow, rather older, with a good
cook and a well-run house. And I actually had my
eye on the widow … Meanwhile I did everything to
help the transition—lent him money to ease his
conscience, introduced him to pretty women to make
him forget his vows. But nothing would do him: he
had but one idea in his beautiful obstinate head. He
wanted the laurel and not the rose, and he kept on
repeating Gautier's axiom, and battering and filing at
his limp prose till he'd spread it out over Lord knows
how many hundred pages. Now and then he would
send a bucketful to a publisher, and of course it would
always come back.

At first it didn't matter—he thought he was 'misun-
derstood'. He took the attitudes of genius, and when-
ever an opus came home he wrote another to keep it
company. Then he had a reaction of despair, and
accused me of deceiving him, and Lord knows what. I
got angry at that, and told him it was he who had
deceived himself. He'd come to me determined to
write, and I'd done my best to help him. That was the

extent of my offence, and I'd done it for his cousin's sake, not his.

That seemed to strike home, and he didn't answer for a minute. Then he said: 'My time's up and my money's up. What do you think I'd better do?'

'I think you'd better not be an ass,' I said.

He turned red, and asked: 'What do you mean by being an ass?'

I took a letter from my desk and held it out to him.

'I mean refusing this offer of Mrs Ellinger's: to be her secretary at a salary of five thousand dollars. There may be a lot more in it than that.'

He flung out his hand with a violence that struck the letter from mine. 'Oh, I know well enough what's in it!' he said, scarlet to the roots of his hair.

'And what's your answer, if you know?' I asked.

He made none at the minute, but turned away slowly to the door. There, with his hand on the threshold, he stopped to ask, almost under his breath: 'Then you really think my stuff's no good?'

I was tired and exasperated, and I laughed. I don't defend my laugh—it was in wretched taste. But I must plead in extenuation that the boy was a fool, and that I'd done my best for him—I really had.

He went out of the room, shutting the door quietly after him. That afternoon I left for Frascati, where I'd promised to spend the Sunday with some friends. I was glad to escape from Gilbert, and by the same token, as I learned that night, I had also escaped from the eyes. I dropped into the same lethargic sleep that had come to me before when their visitations ceased; and when I woke the next morning, in my peaceful painted room above the ilexes, I felt the utter weariness and deep relief that always followed on that sleep. I put in two blessed nights at Frascati, and when I got back to my rooms in Rome I found that Gilbert had gone ... Oh,

nothing tragic had happened—the episode never rose
to *that*. He'd simply packed his manuscripts and left
for America—for his family and the Wall Street desk.
He left a decent note to tell me of his decision, and
behaved altogether, in the circumstances, as little like
a fool as it's possible for a fool to behave …'

IV

Culwin paused again, and Frenham still sat motionless, the dusky contour of his young head reflected in
the mirror at his back.

'And what became of Noyes afterward?' I finally
asked, still disquieted by a sense of incompleteness,
by the need of some connecting thread between the
parallel lines of the tale.

Culwin twitched his shoulders. 'Oh, nothing became
of him—because he became nothing. There could be
no question of 'becoming' about it. He vegetated in an
office, I believe, and finally got a clerkship in a con-
sulate, and married drearily in China. I saw him once
in Hong Kong, years afterward. He was fat and hadn't
shaved. I was told he drank. He didn't recognise me.'

'And the eyes?' I asked, after another pause which
Frenham's continued silence made oppressive.

Culwin, stroking his chin, blinked at me meditatively
through the shadows. 'I never saw them after my last
talk with Gilbert. Put two and two together if you can.
For my part, I haven't found the link.'

He rose stiffly, his hands in his pockets, and walked
over to the table on which reviving drinks had been set
out.

'You must be parched after this dry tale. Here, help
yourself, my dear fellow. Here, Phil—'

He turned back to the hearth.

Frenham made no response to his host's hospitable summons. He still sat in his low chair without moving, but as Culwin advanced toward him, their eyes met in a long look; after which, to my intense surprise, the young man, turning suddenly in his seat, flung his arms across the table, and dropped his face upon them.

Culwin, at the unexpected gesture, stopped short, a flush on his face.

'Phil—what the deuce? Why, have the eyes scared *you*? My dear boy—my dear fellow—I never had such a tribute to my literary ability, never!'

He broke into a chuckle at the thought, and halted on the hearth-rug, his hands still in his pockets, gazing down at the youth's bowed head. Then, as Frenham still made no answer, he moved a step or two nearer.

'Cheer up, my dear Phil! It's years since I've seen them—apparently I've done nothing lately bad enough to call them out of chaos. Unless my present evocation of them has made *you* see them; which would be their worst stroke yet!'

His bantering appeal quivered off into an uneasy laugh, and he moved still nearer, bending over Frenham, and laying his gouty hands on the lad's shoulders.

'Phil, my dear boy, really—what's the matter? Why don't you answer? *Have* you seen the eyes?'

Frenham's face was still hidden, and from where I stood behind Culwin I saw the latter, as if under the rebuff of this unaccountable attitude, draw back slowly from his friend. As he did so, the light of the lamp on the table fell full on his congested face, and I caught its reflection in the mirror behind Frenham's head.

Culwin saw the reflection also. He paused, his face level with the mirror, as if scarcely recognising the countenance in it as his own. But as he looked his

•

expression gradually changed, and for an appreciable space of time he and the image in the glass confronted each other with a glare of slowly gathering hate. Then Culwin let go of Frenham's shoulders, and drew back a step …

Frenham, his face still hidden, did not stir.